A NOTE TO PARENTS

Congratulations on choosing the best in educational materials for your child. By selecting top-quality McGraw-Hill products, you can be assured that the concepts used in our books will reinforce and enhance the skills that are being taught in classrooms nationwide.

And what better way to get young readers excited than with Mercer Mayer's Little Critter, a character loved by children everywhere? Our First Readers offer simple and engaging stories about Little Critter that children can read on their own. Each level incorporates reading skills, colorful illustrations, and challenging activities.

Level 1 – The stories are simple and use repetitive language. Illustrations are highly supportive.
Level 2 - The stories begin to grow in complexity. Language is still repetitive, but it is mixed with more challenging vocabulary.
Level 3 - The stories are more complex. Sentences are longer and more varied.

To help your child make the most of this book, look at the first few pictures in the story and discuss what is happening. Ask your child to predict where the story is going. Then, once your child has read the story, have him or her review the word list and do the activities. This will reinforce vocabulary words from the story and build reading comprehension.

You are your child's first and most influential teacher. No one knows your child the way you do. Tailor your time together to reinforce a newly acquired skill or to overcome a temporary stumbling block. Praise your child's progress and ideas, take delight in his or her imagination, and most of all, enjoy your time together!

Mc Graw Hill McGraw-Hill Children's Publishing

Text Copyright © 2003 McGraw-Hill Children's Publishing.
Art Copyright © 2003 Mercer Mayer.

Send all inquiries to:
McGraw-Hill Children's Publishing
8787 Orion Place
Columbus, OH 43240-4027

Printed in the United States of America.

1-57768-829-5

 A Big Tuna Trading Company, LLC/J. R. Sansevere Book

Library of Congress Cataloging-in-Publication Data is on file with the publisher.

1 2 3 4 5 6 7 8 9 10 PHXBK 07 06 05 04 03 02

FIRST READERS

Level 3   Grades 1–2

NEW KID IN TOWN

by Mercer Mayer

Mc
Graw
Hill   McGraw-Hill
Children's Publishing

Columbus, Ohio

4

One day, Gabby and I were playing catch in my front yard.
"Look!" she said.

She pointed to a big moving van that had stopped on our street.
"Let's go see who's moving into our neighborhood."

A boy was sitting on the curb.

"I'm Gabby," said Gabby. "And this is my friend, Little Critter."

"What's your name?" I asked.

"Max," said the boy in a sad voice.

I asked him what was wrong.

"I miss my friends," said Max.

"Come with us and meet our friends," I said.

8

Max told his parents he was going to
the park with us.
Tiger was flying a kite.
"Max, this is our friend, Tiger," I said.
The four of us took turns flying the kite.

9

10

After that, we went to the pool.
Gator was jumping off the diving board.
"Max, this is our friend, Gator," I said.
The five of us went swimming.

Next, we went to the ice cream shop.
Maurice and Molly were eating
ice cream.
"Max, these are our friends, Maurice
and Molly," I said.
The seven of us had ice cream.

13

Then, we went to the comic book store.
Malcolm was reading a comic book.
"Max, this is our friend, Malcolm," I said.
So the eight of us looked at comics.

Finally, it was time to go home.
We walked Max back to his house.
His parents were in the front yard.
Max smiled and said, "Mom and Dad,
meet my new friends!"

Word List

Read each word in the lists below. Then, find each word in the story. Now, make up a new sentence using the word. Say your sentence out loud.

Words I Know
friend
park
kite
pool
ice cream

Challenge Words
moving
neighborhood
curb
parents
comic

Do You Remember?

Gabby and Little Critter introduced Max to their friends all over town. Match each critter to the place where he or she met Max. Try not to look back at the story.

Tiger

Gator

Maurice and Molly

Malcolm

Adding –ing

When a word has an ing ending, it means that an action is taking place right now.

Example: Little Critter is swimming.

When you add ing to most words, you just put it at the end of the word.

eat ⟶ eating

If the word ends with an e, drop the e and add ing.

dive ⟶ diving

If the word has a short vowel sound, double the last consonant and add ing.

sit ⟶ sitting

20

Read the words in the first column. Then point to the word in each row that shows the correct way to add ing.

write ⟶ writting   writing

walk ⟶ walking   walkeing

dig ⟶ digging   diging

smile ⟶ smilling   smiling

read ⟶ readding   reading

celebrate ⟶ celebrating   celebratting

Logical Reasoning

Read the clues below to figure out in which state Max used to live.

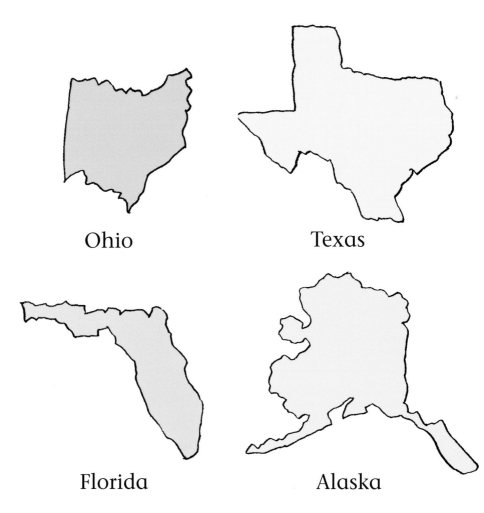

Ohio

Texas

Florida

Alaska

Clues
The state has more than 4 letters in its name.
The state has fewer than 7 letters in its name.
The state has an "e" in its name.

Contractions

Sometimes we put two words together to make one shorter word. The shorter word is called a contraction.

Examples:

let us	⟶	let's
who is	⟶	who's
what is	⟶	what's

Look at the words in the first column. Then point to the correct contraction in the same row.

can not ⟶ cann't   cant'   can't

did not ⟶ didn't   din't   didnt'

I am ⟶ I'am   I'm   Im'

we are ⟶ we'ere   w're   we're

you are ⟶ you're   y'ar   youer

Answer Key

page 19
Do You Remember?

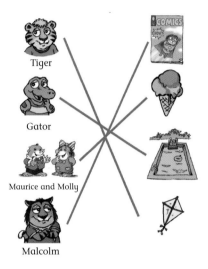

Tiger

Gator

Maurice and Molly

Malcolm

page 21
Adding -ing

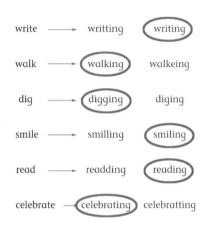

write ⟶ writting (writing)

walk ⟶ (walking) walkeing

dig ⟶ (digging) diging

smile ⟶ smilling (smiling)

read ⟶ readding (reading)

celebrate ⟶ (celebrating) celebratting

page 22
Logical Reasoning

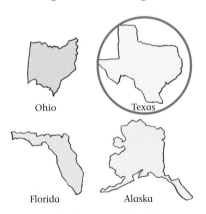

Ohio

Texas

Florida

Alaska

Max just moved from Texas.

page 23
Contractions

can not ⟶ cann't   cant'   (can't)

did not ⟶ (didn't)   din't   didnt'

I am ⟶ I'am   (I'm)   Im'

we are ⟶ we'ere   w're   (we're)

you are ⟶ (you're)   y'ar   youer

24